The Black Bull

Written by Karen McCombie

Illustrated by Eva Dünzinger

Collins

Chapter 1

In a low, dark cottage by a cold, grey lake lived a washerwoman and her three daughters, Kirsten, Mairi and Flora.

Every day was the same; the washerwoman and her girls scrubbed and washed, and washed and scrubbed.

And every day, there were bitter wishes spoken.

"Oh, how I wish I'd fine, strong sons instead of useless daughters!" the washerwoman would snap.

"Oh, how I wish I could escape this place and have adventures!" Kirsten, the eldest, would sigh.

"Oh, how I wish I could find myself a handsome husband!" Mairi, the middle daughter, would moan.

Only the youngest daughter, Flora, stayed silent. But she had her own, quiet wish and it was a simple one – to be happy.

So it went on until one day Kirsten cried, "This dull life isn't for me!"

She packed her few things and left, without a thought for her sisters.

Her mother raged with anger.

Mairi moaned with jealousy.

Flora wept salt tears into the washtub. What would become of Kirsten?

And then a passing shepherd gave them news of her.

Kirsten had wandered for many a day, till she met a wise old woman, who listened as Kirsten spoke of her dreams of adventure.

"Is this one coming now?" asked the wise old woman, pointing back along the road.

Puzzled, Kirsten looked – and saw a splendid coach pulled by six white horses. Inside the coach was a rich lady who loved to roam far and wide, simply to see the wonders of the world. While the rich lady stopped to rest her horses, she asked the wise old woman where she might find a girl to be maid and companion on her travels.

In the blink of an eye, Kirsten stepped into that fine carriage, and into her future.

As soon as the tale was told, Mairi's mind was made up.

"This lonely life isn't for me!" she cried, packing her few things and leaving, without a thought for her younger sister.

Her mother raged with anger.

Flora wept salt tears into the washtub. What would become of Mairi?

And then a travelling tinsmith gave them news of her.

Mairi had wandered for many a day, till she met a wise old woman. She told her of her dreams of a handsome husband.

"Is this him now?" asked the wise woman, pointing back along the road.

Puzzled, Mairi looked – and saw a prettily painted cart pulled by two strong horses. Driving the cart was a handsome farmer. Stopping to let his horses rest, the farmer asked the old woman where he might find himself a good wife.

In the blink of an eye, Mairi stepped into that painted cart, and into her future.

When Mairi's tale was told, her mother raged with anger and Flora wept salt tears into the washtub. What would become of her, now that *both* her sisters were gone?

One chilly morning, as dawn bloomed, Flora whispered, "This troubled life isn't for me," and kissed her mother goodbye as she slept.

Chapter 2

For many a day Flora wandered, till she found herself in a faraway glen, lush with purple heather and green moss, with a stream the colour of amber because of the fine earth from which it sprang. And there she met a wise old woman and told her of her simple hope of happiness.

"Will *this* make you happy?" asked the wise old woman, pointing back along the road.

Puzzled, Flora looked – and gasped.

Charging towards them was a terrifyingly huge, snorting black bull.

"This can't be!" Flora said, backing away from the monstrous beast.

But in the blink of an eye, she was hoisted upon the bull's broad back, and set off into her future.

As the great creature plodded on to who knows where, Flora wept and wept. But slowly the tears stopped, as she rocked peacefully on the bull's sleek black back.

For hours they journeyed, through forests, up hillsides, across rivers, with views so beautiful that Flora sang for the sheer joy of it. The beast liked the sweetness of her voice, for his ears twitched backwards to hear her better.

Then as night fell, the beast brought them to a grand castle. He hammered at the huge wooden door with one of his enormous horns.

The servants of the castle came, bowing low to the bull, as if they knew him. Flora was too timid to ask how that could be, so she stayed quiet and was thankful of the warm fire and cosy bed she was shown to.

She'd never known such comfort, but Flora couldn't enjoy it, not when she looked out of her bedroom window and saw the bull alone in the field below.

In the morning, one of the servants pressed an object into Flora's hand. It was carved to look like an apple and painted green like spring moss.

"Keep this safe," she was told. "You may need it when your heart is sore."

Flora didn't understand, but tucked the object away, as she set off once again, on the back of the great black bull.

Another day passed, of peaceful swaying and contented singing. And once again, come nightfall, the black bull rode up to a grand castle. The castle servants here also bowed low and Flora found herself a guest in another comfortable bedroom. But when she thought of the black bull, taking his lonely rest outside the castle walls, sleep wouldn't come.

In the morning, one of the servants rushed to her.

"Please, take this; it may help if ever your heart is breaking."

It was an object made to look like a pear, painted the colour
of pale amber. Flora tucked it away and let herself be helped
on to the back of the patiently waiting black bull.

The third day was as pleasant as the first two and, as evening fell, they arrived at the most grand castle yet, where more servants bowed to the bull and cared kindly for Flora.
But, again, she couldn't sleep, knowing the bull stood outside, all by himself.

Chapter 3

Next morning, as the creature started on his plodding way, Flora found that an object which looked like a purple plum had been slipped into her pocket. A note attached read: *Keep this by you, for when your heart is in pieces.*

Flora frowned. What did these strange gifts mean?

She frowned again when she saw they'd reached a dark
and forbidding glen of rocky cliffs, raging rivers
and tangled forests. In the distance, the howls of
wolves echoed.

She frowned even more when the black bull stopped –
and his low snorting was replaced with a deep,
booming voice.

"Flora," the black bull spoke, "all is not as it seems. *I* am not as I seem."

Flora slipped down from the creature's back, to see his face better.

"When I was last here, a terrible wrong was done to me, by the greedy ruler of this place," the deep voice rumbled.

"What happened?" asked Flora. Full of wonder and concern, she took the bull's great head in her hands. His eyes were soft brown, so gentle for one so powerful.

"The ruler of the glen is greedy and wants more lands for himself. He ordered me to give my brothers' castles to him, but I would not. He said I'd suffer for my stubbornness."

Flora understood; the castles they'd visited belonged to his family and because he wouldn't hand them over, the bull had been transformed. But from what? Before she could ask, the black bull spoke again.

"I found myself much changed and sent far and away. But now I'm here and must do battle, so as to return to my old life and my future."

"What can I do to help?" asked Flora.

"You've already helped. Your kindness and company have made me strong, Flora," said the beast, "and now all you can do is watch and wait. If this grey sky turns blue, you'll know I've won and will come back to you. If it turns red ... "

Before Flora could beg the bull to explain, he thundered off.

"Take care!" she called after him, but her words were lost in a whooshing, whining wind that sprang from nowhere.

And so Flora pulled her thick shawl around her and huddled under the shelter of an old tree.

Chapter 4

Flora stood and watched, waited and wondered, but the grey sky turned neither blue nor red ... instead, a snowstorm raged, turning the sky – and the glen – pure white.

Chilled to the bone, Flora waited for her black bull, but he never came. She waited till she was so weak that she knew she must find help, but when she tried to climb the glassy, ice-covered cliffs, she slipped and fell.

Desperate, Flora felt for the objects she'd been given in her skirt pocket. Could they help her now? She felt they couldn't. After all, her heart wasn't sore, nor broken, nor in pieces. For the sky hadn't turned red, so somewhere, somehow, her black bull *must* be safe!

Chapter 5

With this happy, hopeful thought, Flora found thorny branches to wrap around her worn boots, so that her every step bit hard into the glassy cliffs.

After many hours' climbing, she escaped that dreadful frozen place. She looked down into the next glen, which was lush with purple heather and green moss.

She followed an amber-coloured stream down towards
a cottage, where a woman in a headscarf was bent over
a washtub. For a fleeting moment, Flora thought of
her mother and sisters, but it wasn't *them* that she longed
to meet again ...

"Pardon me, but have you seen a black bull come this way?"
Flora asked, as she came near.

The woman hadn't, but convinced Flora to stay till she was rested. Flora was grateful, but offered to do chores in exchange.

"Very well, try to clean that," said the woman, pointing to some stained linen in the washtub. "A knight is staying here. He's injured from a battle and half-mad from his wounds. He says whoever cleans the blood from his shirt must be his true love!"

Making no sense of this, Flora rolled up her sleeves
and set to work, all the while softly singing a sad song of
longing. It made tears spring to her eyes – and drop on to
the stained shirt.

"My! Look!" the woman exclaimed,
as she held the dripping, now
unmarked, shirt in the air.

Flora didn't understand the meaning of this, till she heard the woman claim that she'd cleaned the shirt herself. Flora had been tricked!

"So, sir – you'll marry me, since I've cleaned your shirt of blood?" the woman called out.

A young man limped to the cottage doorway and weakly answered "Yes". And in that moment, Flora recognised him.

Shiny black hair, soft brown eyes ... he was her black bull, but he was now human!

He must have won his battle with the greedy ruler, but been so terribly injured he couldn't return to her. So that's why the sky had turned neither blue nor red.

"Dearest black bull, don't you know me?" Flora said urgently, but the knight frowned, shook his head and limped back indoors.

"Wait, please!" Flora called out, her heart sore.

"Leave him be," the woman snapped, barring Flora's way. "He's mine!"

Quickly, Flora reached into her pocket and pulled out the first object she'd been given. A latch snapped open and the two halves of the green apple parted to reveal glimmering emeralds.

"Here, have these, if you'd just let me speak with him!" Flora begged.

The woman snatched the emeralds and stood aside.

Rushing into the room, Flora saw the knight slumped in a chair.

"Don't you remember that you were once a great black bull who took me to your brothers' castles?" she asked him.

"That cannot be," he muttered sadly.

Suddenly, the woman barged by Flora with a cup in her hand. "Drink this for your pain, sir. And I'll send this silly girl away!"

"Wait!" said Flora, her heart in pieces.

She reached for the second object. A latch snapped open and the two halves of the pale yellow pear parted to reveal pieces of precious amber.

"Let me stay a moment more!" Flora begged.

The woman snatched the pieces of amber and left them.

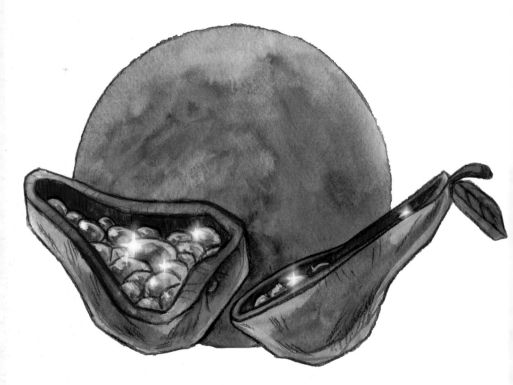

As Flora turned back to him, she saw the knight finish his drink, his brown eyes heavy with sleep.

"Don't you remember telling me to wait and watch for you when you went off to battle?" Flora cried.

But the knight collapsed on the table, in an instant, deep sleep.

At the same time, the woman stormed back in. "Now *leave!*" she ordered.

"Please!" said Flora, her heart breaking.

She reached for the third object. A latch snapped open and the two halves of the purple plum parted to reveal rare lilac sapphires.

"Let me sit awhile as he sleeps!"

The woman shrugged carelessly and took the gems.

Flora went to lift the empty cup from the hand of the knight ... and sniffed. The scent was strong; it was a herb known to make people sleep. She'd been tricked again!

Chapter 6

"Oh, my beloved black bull!" Flora cried. Then she began to sing softly, tears spilling on to the knight's still face.

Flora's tender tears and sweet song made an amazing thing happen.

"Look, he wakes!" said the woman, who now appeared and pulled off her headscarf — revealing herself as the kindly, wise old woman from Flora's first wanderings in the world.

"Flora!" said her black bull knight, taking her in his arms. "My true love!"

It was then that Flora saw she'd been tested, not tricked.

She wasn't selfish, like her sisters.

She wasn't swayed by comfort and riches.

She knew love was measured in care and kind acts and not in a handsome face.

And Flora's heart ached again – but this time with happiness ...

Transformations!

How I wish I could have adventures!

I wish to be happy.

How I wish I could find a husband!

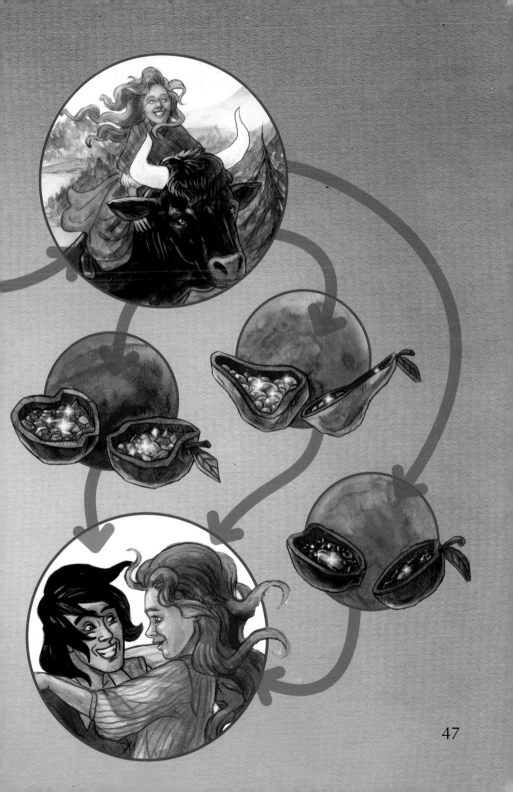

Ideas for reading

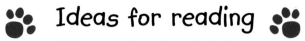

Written by Clare Dowdall, PhD
Lecturer and Primary Literacy Consultant

Reading objectives:
- use dictionaries to check the meaning of words
- discuss their understanding and explain the meaning of words in context
- make predictions from details stated and applied

Spoken language objectives:
- use spoken language to develop understanding through speculating, hypothesizing, imagining and exploring ideas

Curriculum Links: PSHE – health and wellbeing; Art – drawing, painting and other techniques.

Resources: dictionaries; art materials; photographs; scrap magazines; ICT for research; pens and paper

Build a context for reading
- Show children the image on the front cover and read the title. Ask what children know about bulls and their behavior.
- Create a word bank of vocabulary to describe the bull in the cover illustration, e.g. monstrous, immense, beastly, ferocious. Find definitions for these words using a dictionary.
- Ask for a volunteer to read the blurb. Challenge children to look for clues in the blurb and illustration about the origins and setting for this story.
- Look closely at what Flora is holding. Ask children to suggest what it is and how it might feature in the story.

Understand and apply reading strategies
- Read pp2–3 to the children. Help them to make a personal connection to the story by asking what they'd wish for.
- Take turns to read aloud and complete the first chapter. Support children to read with expression, developing characterful voices.